Clint Faraday
book thirty four
Bored to Death

Clint and family are in Cusapín watching the fantastic colorful sunrise over the Caribbean. A tourist comes along the beach to chat, saying she couldn't sleep. She didn't do anything all day yesterday and couldn't sleep. She was bored to death.

Was that one that could be taken literally? When she died, no one cold find a cause.

Of course, it might be that one of the people who she came to get away from who were there to make her life miserable did something.

Clint Faraday
book thirty four
Bored to Death
© 2019 by C. D. Moulton
all rights reserved: no part of this publication may be reproduced or transmitted in any form or by any means, electronic or mechanical, including photocopy, recording, or any other information retrieval system, without permission in writing from the copyright holder/ publisher, except in the case of brief quotations embodied in critical articles or reviews.

This is a work of fiction. Any resemblances to persons, living or dead, or events is purely coincidental unless otherwise stated.

Contents

About the author

CD Moulton has traveled extensively over much of the world both in the music business, where he was a rock guitarist, songwriter and arranger and in an import/export business. He has been everything from a bar owner to auto salvage (junkyard) manager, longshoreman to high steel worker, orchid grower to landscaper, tropical fish farmer to commercial fisherman. He started writing books in 1983 and has published more than 350 books as of January 1, 2023. His most popular books to date are about research with orchids, though much of his science fiction and fantasy work has proven popular. He wrote the CD Grimes, PI series, and the Det. Nick Storie series, Clint Faraday series, and many other works.

He now resides in Gualaca, Chiriqui, Panamá, where he writes books, plays music with friends, does research with orchids and medicinal plants. He has lately become involved in fighting for the rights of the indigenous people, who are among his closest friends, and in fighting the extreme corruption in the courts and police in Panamá.

He offers the free e-book, *Fading Paradise*, that explains what he has been through because of the corruption.

CD is the discoverer of the Chadam Protocol for curing cancer.

Facebook page Ambrosia peruviana for cancer.

Bored to Death

<u>*Sunrise Chat*</u>

Clint Faraday teased at Nito, his one year old son, as they watched the fantastic sunrise over the Caribbean from the porch on his little cabin on the beach in Cusapín, Comarca Ngobe Bugle, Panamá. His beautiful wife, Tyna, brought coffee and sat close. Nito went to run on the beach.

"I think we've found a paradise almost no one ever finds in life," Tyna said, nuzzling at his neck. "No gringo has ever had it so perfect. I think no other Indio has, either.

"We belong together, Clint. I knew it the first time I saw you, when I was sixteen."

"There isn't another place like this. There's certainly no other woman like you. Nito is going to be one of those people who are ridiculously handsome, isn't he?"

They had seen a couple of the Indio mix men that Clint had used the expression about. He'd read it in a book about some director who had sent a man with a message. When the man the message was for opened the door, he said there was a man standing there who was ridiculously handsome. The mix of physical features of Irish-German Clint with the Ngobe features of Tyna could result in such people.

"I hope he'll be like that Lonnie character Dave wrote about."

"You lost me. Lonnie character? Dave wrote about him? In Florida?"

"He wrote a detective series in Florida. Lonnie was a handsome man who lived in cutoffs and did yard work. Women constantly chased him. So did a lot of men."

"I knew he wrote some things in Florida. I never read any of it."

"He gave me a book called *Odd Jobs,* where his detective cop met Lonnie. I translated it to learn English. Lonnie was extremely handsome and a great guy, at the same time, which almost never happens. Nick said that most super-handsome men are assholes."

"I'd ask who the hell Nick is, but I don't really care, even though I agree."

"Nick was his detective. I have you, who's like Lonnie!"

"Except I'm not handsome and I am an asshole most of the time."

"Only when you want to be."

They teased a minute until they heard Nito call

"Coin dega!" the Indio "Good morning!" There was a middle-aged, somewhat heavy, drab woman with frizzy reddish-gray short hair coming along the beach.

She laughed and returned the greeting, plus, "I don't know what it means, but I can figure it! Aren't you a little young to be out here alone on the beach?"

"I'm not!" Nito replied, pointing to Tyna and Clint. He spoke English as well as Spanish and Ngobe. None with accent. He was precocious, to a degree.

She waved at Clint and Tyna and said to Nito, "You're a little doll! You'll be a real lady killer when you're a little older."

She came to offer her hand and say, "Bibi Janes, and no silly puns, please!"

"Puns?" Tyna asked. "Clint and Tyna and Nito Faraday Santos."

"The old picture. *Whatever Happened to Baby Jane?*" she replied. "I guess you never heard of it, here."

"I saw it way back when I was a kid," Clint answered. "My people here don't even watch much TV. Life isn't so much in fantasies. We're living in one."

She laughed. "For you. For me, I'm bored to death! I'm a city person. Business and noise and pressure are my medium. I came here to get away from it, but find it's what I need. If it weren't for a bunch of leeches and hangers-on, I'd be back in Houston. I'll probably go to Panamá City in a couple of days. It has the noise and pressure and impersonality of any big city.

"*That*, I'll miss! The people here stop and talk to a perfect stranger and make one feel welcome. Back home, you never start a conversation with a stranger. If someone wants to chat, there, you're suspicious as hell! I wish there was some way to have both things."

"David," Tyna said.

"David? David who? I don't ... oh. The city. I've heard it's different."

"It's a big city that's more like an overgrown puebla. People stop and chat with strangers, you can leave a kid the size of Nito in the parque while you shop and he's perfectly safe. It also has highrises and casinos and great restaurants and discos and so forth. Two or three shopping malls. Great hospitals," Clint explained. "I don't like cities, but I do like David. Very much.

"Panamá is different."

"You can say that, again! I've traveled all over Europe and Asia and parts of Africa and Australia. There's no place quite like it!" she replied. "I just love these people! They don't make any demands.

They're willing to meet anyone half way. They accept you for what you are.

"I also like that none of the Indigenous people beg. The Latins and blacks in Bocas did, but never an Indigeno!

"It's pretty damned smart! I'd give the children, Indigeno children, coins, on general principles. The others, no way José!"

"We don't beg. If you go to Panamá City or David, they will. Ngobe don't!" Tyna said.

"When I gave them money in Bocas, they always wanted to clean my shoes or give me a trinket. I noticed they don't want something for nothing. I wish my business was ... I came here to get away from that bunch. Sorry."

"Do you have any interests that can be found here?" Tyna asked. "Fishing or surfing or diving? Exploring the forests is fun."

She laughed. "Can you picture me surfing? I simply can't get interested in outdoor things. I like plants, but grow them in a hothouse. Orchids and tropicals. I only swim in pools, though I did swim here in the surf. Very nice!"

"The coastal forests are covered with orchids. Look around right here! We have several hundred species of orchids in the trees and planted around the place," Clint said.

"I noticed them when I came off the beach. I

have some of them. *Catasetums* and the *nodosas.* Not so lush, but I can't give them this climate."

"Dave brings them here. He studies them in the jungles. He only takes those that are on a fallen tree or something where they won't survive, if left," Tyna said. "He's a botanist and musician who goes into the jungles where no white man has ever been. He finds some new ones. I think he wrote a book or two about orchids."

They chatted for awhile. Bibi was a pleasant sort of person. She owned some kind of business and came to escape the constant pressure from her employees and family. No matter what she did, someone would find fault. They all had their schemes and plots. She just wanted to make a living, they wanted to get rich. Most of them didn't care how.

"My own son and daughter are that type. They got it from their father. He started it and didn't have a gram of ethics or morals about him. My father was like that. When they died, they didn't take a dime with them. Dad would screw his own mother out of a few hundred bucks with some phony scheme. In fact, he did! If he knew I'd given it back on the sly he would probably have divorced me.

"Outside of what he called business, he was an average good man."

She went back into the village after a cup of the coffee Tyna grew and dried and ground. It was delicious. Bibi said she could package it and sell it in specialized coffee shops in Houston for six dollars a cup. Tyna laughed and said, "No thanks! I'd end up running away, like you did! I wouldn't miss the pressure. I'd never come back."

They parted friends. The one concession to so-called civilization Clint made here was having a cellular. She bought one when she first came to the country and didn't give but four people the number. She gave it to Clint and Tyna. Nito went along the beach with her until they were almost out of sight of the house, then came back.

"She's a good woman. I think she would like David," Tyna decided.

"She won't stay. She'll go back. It's the life she was raised to," Clint argued. "It's sad, but there isn't anyplace on this world where she can have it all. She wants diametrically opposed things."

"Well, she can stay away from that stuff for awhile, here."

"Clint! Phone! Bibi!" Tyna called.

He went in to say, "Coin dere! How are things with you?"

"They were better than they've ever been until five minutes ago, Clint. The boat just came in. My son and daughter and an accountant for the firm got off! They don't know I saw them. I want to know if you know of a place I can get to where they can't find me. I came here to get away from that!"

"You can stay at Moma's place. She's living there, alone. She would welcome the company," Tyna said. Clint had the phone on speaker.

"I'll come to the hostel and distract them. You can go out the back. Tyna will be there. She can take you to Moma's place. I think you'll like her. Fifteen minutes."

"I'm not there. The man in front will tell them I'm staying, but I'm out. I can't go back for my things, but there's not much that I'll miss."

"Nando will let them think I'm the cleaning girl. I'll get your things for you," Tyna said. "Tell Clint the room number and he can meet you somewhere and take you to Moma's."

She said she'd meet Clint at the little place that has the great chicken soup and patacones.

Clint took Nito. They strolled into town and past the hostel. He saw a gringa in an expensive beach suit on the porch. He nodded to her. Tyna kissed him and Nito, then went inside. Clint smiled, said hello to people he knew, and strolled casually on. He met Bibi at the stand and took her to Moma's, who welcomed her warmly and said she had two whole rooms nobody was using. She was glad to have company. Clint said there were some unwelcome visitors in town. They must not know Bibi was there. It would be handled.

Clint went back into town after about an hour. There were two large black garbage bags by the back door to the hostel he took around the corner and behind the house, there. Estevo would take them to Moma's.

Clint went to the hostel and in the front. There were two overdressed gringos and the gringa at the desk, arguing heatedly with Nando, who was pretending he didn't speak English and that his Spanish wasn't very good. The gringa was livid.

"What's the problem, here?" Clint asked. "Other than the fact that you've come to a country where Spanish is the spoken language and now onto the comarca where Ngobe is spoken and are making silly demands in English.

"What do you want?"

"We have to speak with Bibi Janes," one of the men said. "We know for a fact she's here. He won't tell us which room."

"Number one, she's not here anymore. Number two, Nando won't give you information about any guests here, the same as he won't give anyone information about you. It simply isn't done on the comarca. People don't come here from the states, much. Those who do are usually getting away from a bad situation or person. You're guaranteed privacy in certain matters. We operate only under comarca law, not Panamanian."

"Even when the person sought is a criminal?" the woman asked, acidly.

"Are you claiming that this Bibi person is a criminal? And yes, even a criminal, somewhere else. They aren't necessarily criminals here."

"She ran away with the major control of a large company!" she replied. "Yes, in my personal opinion, she's a criminal!"

"How in unholy hell could anyone run away with control of a company — unless they were the controlling owners?"

"She is," one of the men answered.

"So? She's no criminal if she simply left and took her voting rights with her. If she didn't leave you any voting proxies, there's probably damned good reason."

"We're working on a deal where we can sell a lot of the company for a very good profit and merge with another that has a patent we want. It will profit more than two million dollars per year, minimum. You can see why we can't allow her to simply run off like this!" he said, haughtily.

"Oh? You have to 'allow' her to take a vacation now and then?"

Tyna came to them. Clint kissed her and said he would introduce her to these gringos, but they hadn't the social graces to introduce themselves to him. In Spanish. It might be a good idea to let them think she didn't speak English. She took Nito and left.

"Who was that?!" one of the gringos exclaimed. "My God! What a beauty!"

"My wife. I would have introduced you, but you didn't bother to introduce yourselves. Among the Indigenos, to not introduce yourselves means you don't want to be introduced to anyone else."

"Oh! Sorry! I'm Mr. Janes, this is Mr. Wells, this is Miss Janes, my sister."

"*Mr.* Faraday. Bibi Janes is your mother?"

"Yes," the gringa answered. "We have to talk to her. She has to go back home until we handle the business. I'm sure you can understand that three million dollars is a very large sum of money. She has to take responsibility."

"'Large sums of money' is relative. Maybe she doesn't think it's worth the trouble. I spoke to her once. She seemed to be a responsible type. She seems to already have what she wants and needs. Maybe she doesn't want more."

"She never considers what others need!" Wells snapped. "You can't even begin to understand the importance of money in today's world, living in a primitive jungle among savages!"

Clint stared at him hard for a moment. He hissed, "You'd better take care of what you say about my people and our home, you half-assed stupid bastard son of a bitch. Your piddling three million dollars doesn't mean shit to me or to these people. I can buy and sell the bunch of you with pocket change.

"You can get the hell off of the comarca. Your type of sordid slimy shit-eaters aren't welcome visitors here. We can, and will, see that you don't come here again. I can see why Bibi got away from you. You're pathetic!"

Basilio, head of the council and close friend of Clint, had come in just before this and had heard it. He stepped up to say, "Clint, my brother, I will demand as council chief that these culebras go. Today. And that they never again return to the comarca."

"Who do you think you are?!" Wells demanded. "We represent a very powerful company. We go where we please! No bum without a pot to piss in or a window to throw it out of is telling *me* what to do!"

"He's the chief of the comarca. His word is law," Clint said. "Get the hell out! Now!"

"Also, this bum with no pot or window has donated hundreds of millions of dollars to us, his people, for schools and hospitals," Basilio said, calmly. "The only savages here are you three. We seldom see gringos so greedy and crass."

"He donated *hundreds of millions*?!" Miss Janes cried. "You meant hundreds or maybe ... no! He doesn't have hundreds of thousands, much less hundreds of *millions*! You don't even know what a million is!"

"You are a total embarrassment, Sylvia!" Bibi snapped, coming into the room. She had been just outside the door for about five minutes. Clint had seen movement there, but didn't know it was her. "You have no pretense at class.

"Clint, I decided I will not hide from them. It's heartening to note Basilio ordered them off the comarca.. It means I may stay here for a pleasant vacation.

"Justin, you and your sister and Billy Wells are

unwelcome visitors. Go back to the states. I will return when I get damned good and ready!

"Clint, Moma is a wonderful person! I'll stay with her for a few days, then go to see if David is as great a place as you say.

"Sylvia, that outfit would be stunning on the Riviera or somewhere among that type. Here, it's pretty damned silly. Justin, you are dressed just right for a formal dinner with the captain on a cruise ship. Here, you're ridiculous.

"Billy, you're ridiculous anywhere.

"Goodbye, dear son and daughter. Please come back when you can't stay so long!"

"They can come back to David. They will not come here again," Basilio said.

"You, I like!" Bibi said. "Can I buy you a beer and try to seduce you? Hmmm?"

"Why not?" Basilio replied. They walked out together. Sylvia was looking shocked.

"You'd better be leaving right away. You don't want to be on the water after dark," Clint said.

"I'll leave when I'm ready!" Wells spat.

"Well, you'd better get a thing or two straight," Clint replied, easily. "This is the comarca. The laws of Panama or wherever don't apply. Basilio is the law here. He's said to leave today. If you don't go, he can do whatever he wants, which includes having you executed.

"Got it?"

He walked out. They were all looking shocked.

They did get the boat and paid extra for a trip that wasn't planned. Clint went home to his wife and child.

Bibi stayed for four more days, then went to David. They stayed in contact through the cell phone. Bibi loved David, but said she was going to go a couple more places while she was here. Santiago was supposed to be a lot like parts of Texas. It was mostly just cattle country. Las Tablas was supposed to be a good place for a day or two.

She called from each place to say how much she loved this country. She hadn't ever met people so open and friendly, anywhere. It was true there were a few who were thieves and worse, but really less of them than many other places. It seemed anywhere she went in the world when people found she had a little business they acted the same. Greedy empty fools!

She sent little gifts to Nito, saying she wished her own son was half the man Nito was, and Nito was only a year old!

The calls came every day for a few days, then every two days. Bibi was making friends. She was a likeable person. The calls dropped to once a week. She said she loved the places, but was bored too quickly and was starting to get itchy about the business. She lost one phone and called to tell them her new number. Tyna called her every so often. She called twice more, then there weren't anymore for a month.

Clint was a little worried by that. Some of the so-called "business people" she met were nothing more than cheap scam artists. Two had proposed marriage so they could operate in both Panamá and the US. She hadn't turned them down in a manner designed to make friends. Friends like them, she had by the dozen. She was here to get away from them.

Some of them could be dangerous, in ways. Clint suggested she get a good lawyer and make arrangements to protect her business from being raided by them through a scheme with corrupt courts and petty officials. She said she had sense enough to do that as soon as she left Cusapín.

"They try to fool with anything to do with the company, they're in for a real shock!" she said. "That includes the ones in the states."

Still, Clint worried just a little about her. The name "Manicusi" had come up. That could mean some bad things – or nothing. She was savvy about business.

"Clint, I've called Bibi four times. There's no answer. She sometimes leaves the phone in places, but always calls back after a few hours. I'm getting worried."

Clint nodded. The last time she had called she was in Santiago, being romanced by a slick Latin Lover type. She'd said she was having a great time. She knew exactly what was going on. He was great in bed and she was a fat frumpy old woman. Why not enjoy letting them play their game? She could play, as well.

"You're not fat, frumpy or old," Tyna had answered. "Clint is older than you, you're a bit plump, but the men here like bigger women, and you're exactly as frumpy as you want to be!" She had laughed and replied that she was having more fun than she'd ever had before. She intended to see how long she could make it last.

It was a month and a few days later. Her phone wasn't answered. She didn't call.

"I hope she hasn't decided to actually marry her Latin Lover," Tyna said. "She would get tired of him pretty fast and he would accomplish what he was after. He would get a big part of her money."

"No. She took care of that. Maybe he doesn't know he would get half of what she had in her name in the bank. She keeps the account at five hundred dollars for small emergencies and uses a corporate account for everything else," Clint replied.

He called her phone every hour for four hours. The fifth time it was answered – by the police. It seemed Bibi Janes had died in her sleep. The medical examiner couldn't find a reason. She had been in excellent health and condition. Her body was in Mariato, Veraguas. They had her phone and were noting who called. His name was Clint F. Was that Clinton Faraday, private detective from Florida?

"Clint Faraday, Ngobe detective, retired," he answered. "You say she died in her sleep from unknown causes?"

"Clint!" Tyna, who had just come back into the room, cried. This was on speaker.

"Yes. I am Pancho Ramirez. I worked with you in the capital with Estefan Gortas on the Hansing murder. I think this is not murder, but I think it could be. There are things that can cause a person to die that show no trace."

"I think there's no doubt it was murder. I'm in Cusapín. I'll get there as fast as I can. I liked that lady."

"I can have the helicopter pick you up and bring you. You can be here in – an hour to get there – three hours from – four hours. Nothing much will happen in that time, here."

They made arrangements. Clint threw a few things together and played with Nito and Tyna until they heard the police chopper coming in. He went out to the beach where the chopper sat, and was off. This was the new chopper and would get him there in two and a quarter hours.

Mariato isn't well known. It was fairly large and a seacoast kind of place. There were signs of a lot of wealth in the area. The morgue was by the hospital. Pancho met the chopper and had the pilot take Clint's luggage to the hotel. Pancho explained what they knew, that Bibi had been in town about three weeks, was liked, had several men who chased after her, was fairly conservative and obviously much preferred the Indios over the other Panamanians. She loved the children. She often said that her own had turned out to be greedy pigs. She wished she had known about the children and how they were raised here. She would never have had hers in the states. Hers were an embarrassment. Every one of these, a mother could be proud of!

Pancho let Clint read over all the reports. He had everything they knew and was taken into the morgue to see if he could spot anything. Her body was slid out of the cooler and Pancho said he could examine her in any way he was qualified to do.

Clint took one look and said, "I'm qualified to spot one thing, right here and now!"

"Which is?"

"That isn't Bibi Janes!"

"What?! But we have her passport and other identification! They are her picture!"

"Check the prints. This woman looks a lot like Bibi, but there are differences that might not show in a passport photo."

Pancho called the doctor. He hadn't compared prints. This was the only gringo who looked at all like that in Mariato. He apologized and took the prints. They didn't match the passport.

Pancho ran the prints through immigration. The woman was Lillian Beresford, from Ontario. She had gone off the records four years ago. She had come to Panamá on a tourist visa and had never reported again.

"So! Whatever happened to Bibi Janes?" Clint mused. "I'm surprised she hasn't contacted me!"

They went back to the station. Pancho said that her family had been contacted. They had arrived last night. They were staying at a fancy beach hotel. He hadn't had a viewing of the body. They were to view it at one o'clock, tomorrow, after the final arrangements for it to be delivered to Houston, Texas.

"Maybe I'll manage to run into them," Clint said. "I think I'll be very interested in how they react to the fact that body isn't hers!"

Clint went to his hotel, cleaned up, dressed a bit more than he was used to, and went down to the restaurant. He then went to a bar and restaurant across from the beach hotel. The Janes and Wells were sitting at a side table, seemingly having a great time, laughing and joking with a couple of people who spoke reasonable English. Justin was throwing money around, impressing the others. They seemed very much like his type, but were darker.

He moved to where he could hear snatches, just out of their line of sight. It seemed "Frank" and "Jerry" and "Pauline" were talking business of some type. "Mergers" and "Future mergers" and "Stock issue" were the big topic. "Millions" was a word used far more than lesser numbers.

He left after an hour of that noise. This was one bunch who were in for one hell of a shock. From two possible directions.

He went to the hotel and sacked out.

In the morning, Clint went to breakfast, then to walk on the beach awhile. It was nice, but no comparison to Cusapín.

After awhile, he saw a familiar-looking beach suit come from the hotel and move to sit on a chaise lounge, under a palm frond sun shelter. He took out his camera and did a few zoom shots. Soon Wells came to talk to her. He went back to the hotel and she smirked at his back. He seemed very happy. Clint wondered what she had in mind. He had a feeling the accountant was due for a shock or two.

That beach suit nagged at him. He brightened and mumbled, "So! You never went back to the states! You're here and the woman you think is your mother is dead. You have business meetings about mergers and stock issues. Everybody is happy and enthusiastic!

"Oh, do I want to see the looks on your faces at that viewing! I'll get all the answers I can use, then!"

He went back to his hotel and called Tyna. He told her what was going on.

"They killed the wrong woman and don't know it," Tyna agreed. "I think even I'd like to see their silly faces when the wrong body shows up at the morgue!"

They chatted a bit, then he talked for a minute

with Nito.

He went to the police station to discuss things with Pancho. They made plans for cameras with audio to be there at the viewing.

"They didn't want a fast cremation. That means they think it's her. One or all of them had her killed or killed her themsel ... no. It would be her in that case. They hired a hit man who hit the wrong person.

"Pancho, she had Bibi's passport and Texas driver's license. What other ID?"

"That was all. Normal things in her purse."

"So. Bibi will be damned scared about now. I want to let her know I'm here, but don't have a clue as to how."

"I thought of that as soon as you said the body was the wrong one. There's an interesting little article in *Visitante* this morning." He tossed a copy to Clint.

Mystery Death in Mariato

A woman has died mysteriously in her sleep in a hotel in Mariato, Veraguas. Police cannot find a cause for her death. Famous detective Clint Faraday has gone to Mariato to assist the police in their ongoing investigation. Family members from EE.UU. will arrive today.

"It will tell her you are here. Perhaps she will know you will discover that the body is not her.

Perhaps she will contact you.

"Clint, this woman had her passport. That tells us something, though I do not know what."

"It tells us she was afraid, for some reason. I have to talk to her to get the details."

Pancho nodded. "I have to go to another crime, now. I will see you at ten minutes before one o'clock at the morgue?"

Clint nodded and shook his hand.

Clint went out and to the picturesque little parque, where he wandered around for a few minutes, then headed for a local restaurant for hojaldres and coffee and to listen to a little of the local gossip. Not much was happening, so he went back to the beach. His cellular buzzed when he was on the beach.

"Clint? Bibi. Can't talk. Four o'clock. Renee's. Beto," She rang off.

He walked around the area for awhile. On the outskirts of the town on a badly kept road was a little kiosco called Renee's Refrescos.

He went back to his hotel and cleaned up, then went for a snack at the restaurant. He was outside the morgue at ten to one. Pancho arrived just as he did. He pointed to the door. Sylvia Janes passed the little glass window. Clint grinned and said, "She called me. Later."

Pancho nodded. They went in.

Justin and Sylvia were there. Justin was wearing the same formal suit he'd worn in Cusapín. Clint smirked at them. They showed some shock and disbelief that he was there.

Dr. Somas came to wave them into the cool room. He went to the drawer. Sylvia took a deep shuddering breath. Somas slid the drawer open and drew back the cover sheet.

"GHEEE! What the *hell*? That's the wrong person! That's not my mother!" she screeched. Justin passed out. Clint raised an eyebrow at Pancho, who was having a hard time not to show any reaction.

Somas closed the drawer and looked a question at Pancho, who said, "We seem to have a bit of a mystery here, would you say?"

"I'd say something like that," Clint agreed.

Somas waved ammonium salts under Justin's nose. He sat up and looked around in confusion, then got shakily up. "What happened?" he asked.

"How original!" Sylvia spat. "It's not mother!"

"But ... then ... who is she?" He looked at Pancho.

"A woman from Ontario, Canada. A Lillian Beresford," he replied. "We are most interested in learning how she got your mother's passport and driver's license. Was she given them, or did she steal them? Why hasn't your mother come forward? Yes, we have a few mysteries."

"It's such a shock! I can't think!" Sylvia wailed. "I must have some time to straighten it out in my mind!"

"Very well. We will meet at the station in the morning. Nine o'clock sharp. I will require some answers. I have to decide which questions to ask. Your Mr. Wells will also be there."

They went their separate ways. Clint said he'd be in touch, later. He went out just behind Justin and Sylvia. Wells was waiting on the sidewalk and noted their expressions. "What happened?!" he demanded.

"It isn't mother! Oh, God! It isn't mother!" Sylvia cried. Wells staggered. Justin looked like he would cry. He was terrified.

Clint went on. He wished he could be where he could hear and see what they did, now.

Clint strolled casually around the little parque at three thirty until he spotted the follower. He wandered over to a little stand that sold grilled salchichas and around the side. The follower couldn't see him there. He waited until he saw him through the leaves of a big hibiscus and went to the far side. When the follower had time to get to the side he went quickly across the parque to stand behind the statue. The follower came around the side of the stand. He didn't see him anywhere. He could only have gone down the side street back there, so the follower ran back that way. Clint went along the buildings by the parque and down a certain little street, then turned into the rough rocky road out of town. He was at Renee's at five to four. There were several people there. One was a very handsome Indio. He went to him and said, "Beto?"

"Yes?"

"I am here because Bibi said to meet you here." In Ngobere.

"That is Ngobere. I don't speak much of it. You

are Clint?"

"Yes."

"Will you come with me to Tebario?"

"Yes. Where is Tebario?"

"It is ten kilometers toward the interior."

"Lead on!"

"We will take a bus."

"If we can take it where someone here won't see us."

"We can catch it past Mariato. To see us, they would have to be on the bus."

"Worth a try!"

They chatted a little. Clint asked if he was a gigolo for Bibi.

"Yes. We have great fun and do not lie about it. She tells me she has a lot of money and says I am worth more than I cost. I would ask her to marry me, but she is beyond the age when she can bear children. I wish to be a father. I didn't think I would love her, but I do. We will be more than friends forever. She will return to the United States. I do not want to go there."

They chatted as they waited for the bus. Clint didn't like the feeling as the bus approached and they stepped back into the forest until it passed. They talked awhile longer. There was a bus every half hour. They caught the next one.

Bibi was waiting at the terminal, such as it was

(in front of a Chinese food store). They they went to a house where she and Beto were staying. She had lost a little weight and was taking better care of herself. Beto insisted she take care of herself, but liked a slightly plump woman. They compromised that she wouldn't lose anymore weight. She was actually attractive when she wanted to be. They joked about Bibi calling him her Latin Lover, seeing he wasn't Latin. He was seven eights Indigeno and one eighth Egyptian. That explained his classically handsome features.

She said she had to know what happened to Lily – and was she really murdered?

"I think definitely so. They have some poisons that leave no trace and are probably a pleasant way to die. You get sleepy and a little euphoric, go to sleep and never wake up.

"What about how you knew her and what were you doing?"

"I met her on the bus to Mariato. She got on in Atalaya, same as me. She said she'd seen me in Santiago, but didn't have a chance to talk to me. She thought it was a great coincidence that I was on the same bus, going to the same place as her! We could be sisters!

"She gave me a story about being here because she had a husband who beat her in Canada. She came here to lose herself. It had worked. She was able to get along for very little here and could always find work anywhere she went. She was into real estate.

"Beto was with me, of course. She said she was jealous that I'd found such a gorgeous man. We joked about it.

"Anyhow, I didn't know that my passport was missing until I was checking into the hotel. Luckily, I carry several copies, so it wasn't a big problem.

"I saw Billy Wells the next day in the parque. He was sitting on a bench studying everyone who came by. I told Beto, he said he knew some of the people here, we came here.

"Lily, apparently, knew someone in Mariota and was staying with them for two nights, then she would check into the hotel. She had a job waiting for her.

"It didn't occur to me that she was the one who stole my passport – then. Later, it could only have been her. It saved my life, I honestly believe.

"We decided to watch the buses the first two days here. They all stop for the snack shop at the gas pumps. Everyone gets off to stretch their legs and use the toilets and such. The second day, Wells went back to Santiago or whatever.

"We stopped watching them. I was going to move into Mariota, but Beto and I are having so much fun here I decided we would wait until Sunday. I'm planning to go to Texas in two weeks, then might come back here. I want to be with Beto as much as I can, but the business itch is getting bad. I'll be there a month and be sick of it again.

"I was going to drop a bomb on that greedy bunch of slime. I changed all the papers to where Basilio inherits everything if anything happens to me. It's in his name, to be used and managed by the Ngobe Bugle. If they'd known that, maybe Lily would be alive. It's totally legally done and the corporation lawyers will get copies of the papers, soon. Within sixty days, which is about now."

"I see. Did you happen to get any names of the people your kids and Wells were working with?"

"No, not really. They wouldn't know anyone from here. They knew somebody from Colombia, I believe. Rather unsavory type."

"Manicusi?"

"I'm not sure. I might have heard the name."

"Frank Valares? Geraldo Mesas? Paulina Mendez?"

"Mesas? I think that's the Colombian. I thought that was a strange name. Tables, in English. Why?"

"They met with Justin, Sylvia, and Wells in

Mariota. They were having a great time, talking about mergers and stock issues and millions and millions of dollars. The night before the viewing of the body, where Sylvia screeched and Justin fainted."

"So. They were fully expecting to see me there. They've made some kind of agreement where they can get the company. They would enter a partnership with those people and get rich. They saw that they'd killed the wrong person! That must have been a shock!"

"You like understatement as much as I do!"

She laughed. "Wait until they find out they even did that stupidity for nothing. They wouldn't get the company.

"Clint, I don't think they did that. Not Sylvia and Justin, anyhow."

"No, but they wouldn't stop it if Wells made some kind of agreement."

She thought and nodded, then giggled. "They hired someone to do it. He then killed the wrong person. They're the only ones who know who was hired. That person knows that. They've made some kind of deal with gangsters from, of all places, Colombia!

"They're in one hell of a fix, aren't they?"

"Oh, yeah! They made the deal through those hoods and they know which one or ones did the actual hiring. I don't think I'd like to be in their shoes, right about now!"

She shook her head. "All for money, which they already have more of than they can use.

"Clint, I can't let anything happen to Sylvia and Justin. Despite it all, they're my kids."

"Okay. I can see what I can see. Maybe it can be diverted. If Wells was the only one they dealt with directly, Wells is held responsible. It looks too much like a setup to scam ... I have to find who the Colombians work for. That's the only place I can stop it. They'll have a certain amount of time to straighten it out. The Colombians will tell you not to kill the one who owes you too soon. A corpse can't pay."

They talked about it for awhile longer. Clint would try to find who the schemer behind the dreamers was. Their dreams of having all those millions had turned into a nightmare where they wouldn't get anything and were in deep doo-doo on top of it. He would try to put it all on Wells. He was the real schemer from that part. Justin and Sylvia were the dreamers who were going along with the scheme.

He called Tyna. She and Bibi had a great time swapping stories. Tyna was introduced to Beto over the phone. They didn't try to gloss over the fact that he had started out as a paid sex toy and had ended up actual lovers. It was on speaker, so they all got into it.

Clint took the late bus back to Mariota. He would get there after midnight. He wondered if he was missed very much.

In the morning, he went to the police station to discuss some things with Pancho.

Pancho said he had a copy of the old legal will from Houston. The company had sent it for the dispensation of assets and the return of Bibi's body. It was mentioned in the will that, should she die in a foreign country, the company would accept all expenses for returning the body for burial in the cemetery there.

"I think you will find interest in the terms," Pancho suggested. "It seems the people here aren't the only heirs. I wonder if Mrs. Janes is aware of parts of this will."

"We can call her and see," Clint replied. "If you can find connections here of three Colombians with someone besides Wells and the Janes, it might prove most enlightening."

"You found her?"

"She found me. Yes."

"And that's where you were until midnight yesterday?"

"Uh-huh."

"You were seen going along the Oeste road. You didn't come back. I was worried. You are dealing with killers who we don't know."

"It was your follower?"

"Follower? No. I only asked that any officer who saw you anywhere report it."

Clint nodded. He took out his cellular and called Beto's number. He was passed to Bibi.

"Hi. Do you know what was in the will the company had?"

"Will? Oh, yes. All parts of the corporation were to be passed directly to my kids with a codicil that Wells and Hodges get two percent apiece. I can imagine that was altered to twenty percent? That would be typical. It's why my personal lawyer has a copy they don't know about. I have never trusted anyone in that bunch who I couldn't throw over the six story corporation headquarters building left handed."

"No," Pancho said. Clint introduced him. "The part where each stockholder gets a percent based on the amount of control stock they held, and Wells gets a piece of other personal properties and/or funds."

"Well, my personal will, even then, would cut that out. The one I registered two months ago from here makes all personal properties and/or funds property of the Ngobe Bugle in the person of Basilio. What I didn't tell Clint is that he's the one in charge of seeing all terms are met. He gets a whole extra five dollars for the trouble!"

"Clint just gave the phone the finger. I think it would be to your safety to make the new will known."

"Well, maybe that I've changed the will as to disbursement. No details."

They chatted. Clint said he was going to nose around. Pancho would do a thorough check on the Colombians.

It was two and a half hours later. Clint didn't have anything new, so went back to the police station. Pancho called for the records officer to bring in what he had requested. She brought in some files and said immigration would have a report in a few minutes – Panamanian, which could mean a few hours.

Not much. Known contacts among them didn't come up with anything new except that Mesas had met with a lawyer, Antonio Fedricos Juan, in Santiago, several times and in Mariota once – that was known. Fedricos was suspected of handling legal matters for some money laundering people. Mesas was Colombiano. Add it up.

Clint sat back and said, "Pancho, can we get a list of the suspected launderers this shyster is suspected of handling? See who's here?"

"I can try. You're to be given total cooperation. You are certified to receive the interdepartmental memos and so forth, which is to say, 'Sure! Why not?'" He called the records officer in and requested the information. He had to explain that Clint had clearance from Panamá City. She went out and returned in ten minutes with a list. She said that wasn't to leave the office. Everyone agreed.

"That shows it's some biggies. They've paid not to be investigated too much. Standard," Pancho said.

Clint looked over the list. There were eleven names and dates. One stood out to him.

"Paulo Manicusi," he said, pointing. "So. I was wondering when his name was coming up."

"Why?"

"Because it came up in passing more than two months ago. There's always a solid reason such lovely people are mentioned.

"Pancho, we've got to tag that one's ass for something! I've heard of him one time too many, always with some crooked deal that brings in innocent people."

"We can try. With people at his level it's not going to be easy."

"I don't ask for easy. Only for a small break."

Clint's phone buzzed. It was Bibi. He answered.

"Clint? Beto. Bibi is somewhere I may not say over the phone. I am to come to Mariota. I am to tell you that Wells and Mesa are here looking for her. She has gone with friends she can trust, Indios. Even I am not to know where. There is a man who is not from around here who is always close when I look around. I am to do what you say."

Pancho was listening. It was on speaker. "Beto? We have not met. I am Pancho Ramirez, Policía. Is there an officer close?"

"Across the parque. I can see him."

"Wave to him! Call him over!"

They could hear Beto call and waited a minute. Beto said, "He is here."

"Pass him the phone."

There was a slight pause.

"This is Capitan Francisco Ramirez, Policía, Manitos. To whom am I speaking?"

"Roberto Sandoval. I believe I know you from a few years back in Santiago?"

"No. Panonomé. You are with an Indigeno man, Beto. You are to escort him here to Mariota. He is in grave danger. He has a suspected follower he will discretely point out to you. If any move is made toward harming Beto in any way, you are to shoot first and question the corpse later. Clear?"

"Yes. There is a bus in six or eight minutes. The truck is on duty at a disturbance."

"Very well. You should arrive here in a half hour or so. I will meet the bus. You are to trust no one but myself or a man called Clint Faraday."

"I know Clint from Bocas."

"Excellent!"

They waited. Clint said he hoped the follower would be on the bus with them. He was going to answer some questions, like it or not.

"We are not allowed to use force in questioning anymore," Pancho warned.

"*You* aren't. I'm not officially police." Pancho grinned.

They waited forty minutes until the bus arrived. Beto and Berto got off and came to Clint and Pancho. Beto nodded at Clint when a man got off the bus. Berto did the same with Pancho.

"We'll go to the station for a talk, Beto. Will you be long, Clint?"

"I hope not." The three walked toward the station. Clint casually strolled toward the bus stop. The follower soon came toward the station. Clint passed him, noting he was the one who was following him earlier. As they passed, Clint turned and followed a couple of paces behind. The man stiffened a bit and kept moving. Clint waited until they were out of the parque and sight from others to say, "Move straight ahead. Do not turn. Make one wrong move and you will die. I will tell you when to turn and which way."

The man missed a step, then continued ahead.

Clint could see he was reaching into his belt in front or something by the crook in his arm and the fact his arm wasn't swinging anymore.

"If you think you're fast enough, try it."

The arm swung back down. Clint could see something hidden in the long sleeve. He shoved a cigarette lighter hard into the man's back over the kidney and reached around to take the switchblade from the sleeve.

"That was an immensely stupid thing to do. I'm not an amateur, like you. You just lost an option. Turn left into the alley between those two stores." Clint could see the sudden sweat on the back of his neck and the tense way he was moving.

They went a little way into the alley. Clint shoved him into the wall and said, "All I want is the name of the person you work for. You can go. If it doesn't check out, you will. Capiche?"

"He'll have me killed if I tell!"

"And I will if you don't. An unenviable position to find yourself in. I'll arrange that he doesn't know if you're not followed."

There was a pause. "Paulo M. I won't say more. I haven't used his name!"

"Exactly who I thought. Get out of town. Tell him I made you and you managed to get away before you told me anything. I'll come out of here in five minutes and claim someone hit me from behind and tried to take my wallet."

He bolted. Clint hung around and smudged a little dirt over his eye on his forehead and a little on his shirtsleeve. He then went out and stood, looking confused. Estefan, a policeman Clint had met, came over.

"What happened? You're Clint Faraday?"

"I was going through and got hit from behind. I think someone tried to get my wallet!" he pointed casually to behind Estefan. A woman had come up quietly to listen. Estefan didn't react.

"Can you describe who did it? Did you see him enough to identify?"

"No. I was going through. A man was ahead of me. I didn't see anyone else around. He might have turned ... I don't know. I don't remember."

"Well, are you alright?"

"I think so. I've been hit a hell of a lot harder."

Estefan nodded and suggested that Clint file a report. He walked away. The woman had left as soon as he'd said he didn't see who it was.

He went to the station. Pancho and Beto were there. He said, "Who I thought. Manicusi."

"So."

"Don't let it be known, even to your officers," Clint warned. "There's something I don't like, here."

"Which is?"

"Estefan. Did he make any kind of report that anyone was mugged within, say, the last fifteen minutes?"

"No. He came to see if you were alright and what you had learned?"

"Uh-huh. He knew my name."

"All of us know your name."

"There was a woman just behind him. Dark, streaked hair, slim, big boobs, green tight dress."

"Looks Colombiana, in other words."

"Something like that."

Pancho went out. Beto and Clint chatted. Soon, Pancho came back in.

"Irena Velasquez. Samuel says she and Estefan talk a lot. He thinks she is his side piece."

Clint nodded. "And both of them are in the employee or owned by Paulo Manicusi."

"We can use that, I think?"

"We can damned well try!"

<u>*Who Is Tony Mendino?*</u>

The slightly stocky dark man with a bushy mustache and a bit too-long hair got off the bus in Santiago, stuck a cigar in his mouth, lit it and looked around. He took the cigar out of his mouth, made a face, said, "Cheap piece of shit! That ain't no Cubano!" and spit. He flung the cigar into the parking lot.

"Hey! You! Yeah, you. Where's a decent hotel out here in Nowheresburg!?" in a gravelly voice. The girl looked at him and said, "No habla Ingles." She walked away.

"Shit! What's that Pyramid place like?"

"Not bad," a black man standing by a column said. "You from the states?"

"Nah! Well, yeah, but I wasn't born there, even. Norma, Italy."

"I was in Italy once. In the US army. Rome."

"Yeah. Everbody goes to Roma. Anybody but you speak English here?"

"Not many. Spanish shouldn't be too far from Italian."

"Yeah, but I don't know so much Italian. I was a two year old sprout when I was brought to Chi.

My Mom was hit by a damned bus when I was three and they all spoke English and that's all I know. I came here because my boss said to come here and you do what he says.

"Know anybody named Frederico? Some kind of lawyer or wharever?"

"Frederico? You mean Tony Fedrico?"

"Frederico, Fedrico. What's the difference? My name's Tony, too."

"He's a lawyer for what you call the mob here. He has an office on Calle Segundo, close to the local bus terminal. He's not here today. He comes here on Tuesday and Thursday and has an office in San Francisco on Mondays, Wednesdays and Fridays."

"He goes all the way to California three days a week? What? He's nuts!"

"San Francisco is a town just a few kilometers away."

"Oh. Yeah. Right. Where's a good whorehouse? I haven't had any in two weeks and I'm gettin' horny as hell!"

"Any bar after nine o'clock. If they're not there, the bartender can tell you where to find them or can get a girl for you."

"Yeah. That's part of bartendin' anywhere. Get a couple girls on the side. I was a bouncer once. Same thing."

He went to the Pyramid and got a room. An Indio in the lobby looked at him strangely. He'd met him before, but not as Tony Mendino. He'd had an Indio show him why they saw through his disguises so quickly. He'd changed a few things, such as the pattern of blood veins on the backs of his hands. It seemed to work. This one saw similarities, but that was the kind of thing they noted. That was not Clint Faraday to Saldo.

He went to his room and took out his computer to e-mail friends. He also sent a few messages to himself through other e-mails.

He went to dinner and tried to talk with several people, but Tony didn't speak Spanish. He went back to his room to change into more of a suit and spray himself with some loud perfume. He went to a bar and got across to the bartender that he wanted a woman. The bartender sent him to another bar. Wednesdays weren't very good at that one.

He went back to the hotel, later. He didn't go to the other bar, but people at the first one would assume he had.

He sacked out.

In the morning he went to the restaurant by the terminal and talked with various gringos going through on the David and Bocas del Toro buses. He met a couple from Chicago, which he knew very little about. He said he was raised out by the lake. They mentioned a suburb. He said he'd been through a few times, but was from more south.

She stiffened noticeably. They tried to be polite. They soon went to get back on their bus, even though it didn't leave for another twenty minutes. A man from a nearby table was from Detroit. He said he knew Chi and that it wasn't a good idea to let people know he was raised in that section. It didn't enjoy a very good image.

"Yeah. Little Italy. I should'a known, but I didn't think it would matter here. I wasn't there, well not *right* there. I was out a little. The people who raised me weren't even Italian. They're from Romania. I never learnt no Italian."

"But you work for an Italian?" Clint wondered why he was so interested.

"Yeah, sort of. Jew, but partner with a couple."

"Leven?"

"Heard of that one! No. Money Mort."

"I don't ... they call him that?"

"Not to his face. Good way to lose yours."

"Mort Goldberg?"

Clint remembered a name Manny, a good friend ex-gangster don from California had used a few times. "Mort Eisenberger."

"He's from Chi?! I always thought he was from California!"

"He's from anywhere he wants to be from."

He laughed. "I'm Franko Talivero. Detroit."

"I'm Tony Mendino, from hunger, if you believe my stepbrothers. Born in Italy, raised near Chi. I have to remember to say 'near Chi' and not in it. Not what part!"

They chatted a few more minutes. Franko got on the Panamá City bus. As he was getting on, he stopped and asked, "Say! Have you seen Marko Boccini in Panamá?"

Marko Boccini was the man now called Manny Matthews. He was supposed to be, so far as anyone could find, in the Mediterranean on a private island.

"Hah! If I saw him I could make a million with a phone call! I wouldn't be tellin you!"

They both laughed. Franko got on the bus.

Tony went on to the law office of Fedrico. The secretary said he would be in at eleven, but was occupied with a difficult case and wouldn't be taking on more clients for awhile.

"Yeah, yeah. I ain't no damned client. I'm from a client. Mort Eisenberg. Mancini. Manicusi. Wells. That bunch. Somethin' about pickin up a will or one of those things. I don't know from nothin' and don't want to."

"A moment." She rifled through some files. "There's a Wells and a Manicusi on the Janes-

Working Holding ... there is no will ... Mr. Fedrico has it. He and Mr. Wells are going to ... probate ... cancelled. Subject found. Not dead. wrong body ... stolen passport.

"There is nothing here. Do you have a request document to present to Mr. Fedrico?"

"Shit! I'll come back when Tony's here. I didn't come to this half-assed town for nothin', I hope!"

"Very well." He was dismissed.

He went back to the hotel, got his maleta and headed for Mariota. He got a lot more than he was after on this one! It would seem that Billy Wells was the connecting factor, which he'd hoped he could dig out later. Manicusi was in it and had probably arranged the hit on the wrong person. Maybe Fedrico, but it was Manicusi's orders and his deal.

He would arrange with Pancho to tag Wells. He wanted that one, but his main effort was now to get Manicusi out of the picture for good. He had a reputation of involving innocent people in his swindles and getting away with it because he paid off the corrupt officials. He seemed to consider himself untouchable. Clint intended to touch him.

Clint got into Mariota a little after four as himself. He'd gotten off before the town and rode on a vegetable truck to the far side of town, then had come in on the bus from Arenas, as far along the coast as the road went. The bus stopped for a few minutes in Mariota, then went on. Clint managed to talk to people at the stop until it left. Irena Vasquez asked the door boy where Clint got on. The boy was paid to tell her La Loma, a town close to Arenas.

Clint followed her to the restaurant where the bunch hung around. She went to their table to one side, next to a patio with a lot of thick leafy shrubbery where Clint could stay behind undetected. She said Faraday had gotten on the bus at La Loma, close to Arenas. He wasn't in any Santiago. He couldn't have gotten there fast enough to catch the bus back to Mariota.

"He runs around in that police helicopter!" Wells pointed out.

"It wasn't in Santiago and Mendino got on the bus there," Justin said. "I don't know why you're so worried about him or Faraday."

"I wouldn't have to be if I knew who the hell Tony Mendino is! He knew about Manicusi. He was supposed to be sent by some mobsters in California or somewhere. He got off a bus from David and left on one for the capital. Fedrico never heard of him."

"Who is Manicusi?" Sylvia asked. "I know Fedrico is that sleazy lawyer."

"He's a man who arranges ... things," Wells said. "Fedrico works for him sometimes. The mergers were to be handled through him. He'd arranged for the will to be certified, but it wasn't even the right ... it's totally fucked!"

"So? The will wasn't even brought up. Why the big panic because of it? Nobody ever even read it," Sylvia said. "It's not important! Forget it!"

"No, *it's* not important. Us getting a copy sent here isn't important because the police would require it. Fedrico having a copy is important! Damned important! Mendino knew about it. That's a very scary thing for *me*," Wells replied.

"Why?" Justin asked.

"Because we're here. Faraday knows we stayed. That's something you might want to explain? We stay, she ends up murdered? You want to explain that?"

"We stayed to get the company proxies," Sylvia said, waving her hand in dismissal.

"God, you're stupid!" Wells snarled. "If *she* died, we could claim that! *She* can say it was damned plain that we weren't going to get them! There goes your little explanation, right down the toilet!"

"It doesn't prove anything! Don't you ever call me stupid again!"

"You're guilty until proven innocent here,"

Justin said. "I know what you're saying. There's a lot of evidence that we're guilty of something. *They* don't have to prove it. *We* have to *dis*prove it!"

"Give that man the golden ring!" Wells replied. "We are, in the vernacular, fucked, if we can't find that Mendino character or see that he's not here any longer."

"I think we should say we were only here to take our mother's body home," Sylvia said. "We would be out of the country and they couldn't do anything!"

"Oh, sure! We can just leave with a stranger's body that was supposed to be your mother laying there in the morgue like it would be perfectly natural that we would do that – not knowing where your mother is or what happened to her!" Wells said. "We've done and said the wrong thing too many times. That police captain already said we aren't to go until some hard questions are answered."

"Such as?" Justin asked.

"Such as you fainting when the body wasn't your mother! You should have been happy because it wasn't her. Sylvie Darlin' screams that it was the 'wrong person.' Oh, yeah. What kind of questions could they possibly ask?" Wells was snarling again.

"We have to get out of here!" Sylvia cried. "*We* didn't do anything! They can't hold us!"

"But you knew about it, meaning you know who's responsible," Wells pointed out.

"*You* set it all up!" Justin replied, hotly. "You screwed up everything! Don't think I haven't considered what that could mean. Don't think it would work!"

"What...?" Sylvia asked.

"We know. We have to go," he answered.

"That's what I want! I want to get out of here!"

"God, you're stupid!" he said, sadly. "That's not the way you would go."

"*Yeep*!"

"I have to go. Not from you," Wells said. "I'll want some insurance. Manicusi can arrange for the investigation to stop, then we can go, but I'll always be a deadly threat. I know him, I know his methods."

"But he knows he can buy out of anything," Justin put in. "I don't think he'll do anything to you. He'll have to wonder what you've left that could cause him headaches if anything happens to you."

Clint had what he wanted. He had the lever. He went toward the station. He was going to arrange a little unpleasant surprise or ten for that bunch. Particularly Wells.

He thought a bit, then went on and bought a cheap cellular. He didn't doubt Manicusi had found a way to listen to him by now.

He called Beto and made some arrangements. Bibi would meet him later and would make some plans with him.

Clint took the back road and caught the bus out of town. Beto met him and took him into the forest to a little house. An Indigena was sitting on the porch. When they came close, she called to Bibi, who came out from a little bodega near the creek that passed below.

Clint talked awhile with all of them, then he and Bibi went for a stroll along the creek. He told her all they'd found so far. She said that sounded about like she thought where Billy Wells was concerned.

"We can use this stuff to clean this mess up, so far as Panamá's concerned. We have to have a frank little discussion with them. I'd like for you to be there to throw a few lines into the water."

"Don't try for anymore metaphors, Clint. That one missed.

"I'm in! I'm getting bored beyond tolerance now. I want to get back to see what's happening with the business. I do like for it to succeed, but it's not about profit. It's about proving I can.

"Weird, huh?"

"Not really. This is a big part of that. Manicusi

would end up with the whole thing and you'd wonder what happened.

"Not you. Your family and partners."

"I know how it works. It would never happen while I have control. They'd learn the old sow has a few smarts and a few tricks of her own!"

"We'll call for a meeting this afternoon? Four?"

"Sounds like a plan! Go for it!"

Clint went back into town and to the police station half an hour later. He met with Pancho and laid out what he intended doing.

It was two ten. He went to the hotel to clean up. Velasquez was in the lobby. He smirked at her and shook his head, mouthing, "Amateur!" He went up to his room. A few minutes later there was a knock. It was Velasquez. He stood back and she went into the room.

"What?" Clint asked.

"Who is Tony Mendino?"

Clint shrugged and asked why.

"He showed up in Santiago and knows some things nobody's supposed to know."

Clint took out the new throwaway phone and punched a number. It was Pancho. He said he wanted some information about a Tony Mendino. He listened for a minute, then said he'd see him later.

"He's a gofer for a big mobster in California. He

was watched when he was here, but he just went to David, then Santiago, where he went to a lawyer's office, then went to the city and is on a plane for California at the moment."

"Not from Texas?"

"No. California and Chicago."

"Thanks." She left. Clint grinned.

At three forty five he went to the station. Sylvia, Justin and Wells were sitting on straightbacked chairs in the hall. Clint greeted them and went into Pancho's office. Bibi was there. She grinned at him.

Pancho talked for a minute, discussing what they planned and finishing his explanations to Bibi.

Pancho and Clint went out to lead the trio into a little room with a table and chairs. Pancho waved at the table. Wells immediately headed for the head of the table. The rest of them sat around, Pancho and Clint on one side and Sylvia and Justin on the other. Pancho spread out some papers and looked up at Wells, who was lounging back with a superior posture.

"We have a few things to discuss about the dead woman and who is or who might be involved," Pancho began.

"Just one damned minute!" Wells snapped. "Is this a formal police meeting? Then where is the secretary? Why aren't you recording?"

"We can make it formal, but I don't think you'd like that at all," Clint said. "Now, you aren't under any oath. Nobody can find what you've said or done here. If there's a recording, any number of people can listen to it. We don't kid ourselves about the corruption, even in this police department.

"Names are coming up. I very seriously doubt you'd care for those people to know they were even discussed here."

"No recording!" Justin said.

Erma, an officer they could trust, came in to whisper to Pancho. He said, "Arrest him! Now!"

She stepped outside, there were some loud voices and she marched Estefan Lupus in at gunpoint. "He was listening and recording," she said.

"Security. No contacts, even interior. No calls," Pancho ordered. She marched him out.

"As I was saying?" Clint said. "I'll guarantee confidentiality."

"I suspected him of something. He was talking to Irena too much," Wells said. "So. They were checking on us all the time."

"All we want is to know the deal that ended up with Beresford dead," Pancho said. "We aren't stupid. It was transparent that you contracted to have Mrs. Janes killed. We haven't quite figured why, except that it was to enable you to contract merger deals with her company. That leads to knowing who those mergers were with and who arranged things. If it is the same people, it was a scam that would have cost you everything. This isn't the first time this has happened here.

"Velasquez and Lupus are in the pay of Antonio Fedrico. Fedrico is in the pay of several known gangsters and drug cartels.

"We need a name."

"I know Fedrico," Wells said. "I won't say he made the arrangements for several things. I can't say who did."

The door opened as he was saying that. Bibi said, "Does the name Manicusi ring any bells?"

Justin jumped up. His chair fell over. Sylvia was white and staring. Wells showed shock. Bibi sat at the end of the table facing Wells.

"Well?"

"Mrs. Janes, I don't know what to say here. Why do you mention this Mancini person?" Wells asked.

"Pull that shit with someone else! I mentioned him because he was working with Fedrico to scam the bunch of you half-assed morons out of my company. I haven't stayed in business this long because I don't know how that crap works! You went too far when you made a deal with him to knock me over.

"I have a lovely family, Clint. You got to know how lovely back in Cusapín and get it proven here.

"I'll allow you to go back to Texas and clear out of my houses and company if you help us tag those sleazy bastards. If not, you have charges to disprove that will put you in the pen here for fifteen to twenty years. Pancho, here, wants to put this Manicusi hood out of business for that twenty years. Fedrico can go with him!

"Your choice! I don't have anymore loyalty to you than you had to me.

"Wells, this is requested by Clint. He's the kind of person who cares about people, not silly things and money. Personally, I think I'd enjoy hearing how Manicusi handled you!

"Now! You can have thirty days to clear out of the house and properties in Texas or you can go to jail here and answer to your good friends and merger partners!

"Sylvia and Justin. Your father left you half a million dollars apiece. I should take that, too, but maybe you can use it to start a business of your own that your kids can try to have you killed to get!

"Wells, you get fifty five grand severance pay, which will be in payment for your stock. Same with Sylvia and Justin. They keep the money, not the stock.

"If there's nothing else, Pancho? I have the most fantastic lover who's waiting for me."

"Their choice."

"I won't live to get back to the states!" Wells wailed. "No matter what, he can get me!"

"No, he can't," Pancho answered. "He makes people believe that. You can see how efficient his hit men are from this. As Clint says, amateurs!

"I assure you. Manicusi and Fedrico will have far too much to occupy their time than to knock off someone who has already given testimony. All that would do is add to the charges and prove yours at the same time. Things are changing here. No one is untouchable. Anyone who would make a corrupt deal with him will be charged, and they know it. In his particular case, everything is lost in a moment. He is through.

"Miss and Mr. Janes, you need not base your reply on Mr. Wells. You accept the deal or we turn on the recorder and bring in a recording secretary."

"I have it all written down. It's in the hotel safe and on this memory stick." He handed Pancho a memory stick. "I don't think you'll need Billy's testimony. I knew it was thorough or failure."

Pancho called in Erma and said to go to the hotel with the document Justin would give her and bring back everything under his name in the safe.

"It's in the name of Clinton Faraday, but I put it there," Justin said. "I could guarantee it would go to the right place if I were killed."

Erma left. Bibi stood and said she would like to have dinner with Clint one more time before she went back to Texas – in Cusapín.

"Done! Bring Beto. I like him."

She left. They waited ten minutes or so until Erma came back. There was nothing in the hotel safe for Clint Faraday or Justin Janes. Pancho sighed and said he'd be back in ten minutes. He went out with Erma. They came back in ten minutes, but not with anything from the safe. With the cleaning woman. She would testify as to who paid her to take the stuff or go to jail for three years. She gave them Velasquez.

"The lovely Irena boarded the Santiago bus fifteen minutes ago, not carrying anything except her purse and a small maleta. Seems she was upset because something happened at the hotel that would put her cute little ass in a crack," Pancho announced. "She'll be detained as soon as the truck catches the bus."

They printed the pages on the memory stick. They were as thorough as Justin had suggested

"This will put those slimy sons of bitches away for twenty to thirty," Pancho said. "Mr. Wells and the Janes, there is another bus destined for Santiago in three hours. I suggest, pointedly, that you be on it. You can arrange your immediate return to Texas on the computer.

"Well, Clint! We work very well together, don't we?"

"Sure do! I'm going to be on that same bus. I miss my wife and kid!"

"Panamá brought you here in a helicopter. Panamá will return you to your home on that helicopter. Perhaps Mrs. Janes and her gigolo will wish to accompany you. Bien viaje!"

Clint teased at Nito and laughed at Bibi, who had just told a joke about a Texan in Panamá. Beto came up from the sparkling surf and rinsed in the shower. Tyna brought them all lemonade and announced that their dinner of lobster and crab chowder would be ready in half an hour. Be there or do without!.

"Well, Clint. I'm off – no remarks! – in the morning for Texas. I'll be back within a month. I get bored for the business here and will get bored for here very soon there," Bibi said. "I love you, Beto. I know you love me. I hope we'll meet again. We can romp a bit for old time's sake. You aren't like most handsome men I've met. You're really fantastic in bed!

"I would never say things like that in the states. The freedom here is in a lot of areas.

"Tyna, I'm not even jealous because you're so beautiful. You're a fun person. I tried to seduce Clint and can't even pout because it didn't work. The competition's too stiff.

"Nito, you'll have to keep an eye on your father. He'll tend to run off all the time to help the police solve a murder.

"I love you people. I love the Indigenos, yet I'm running off! I'm really fucked up, aren't I?"

"Yep!" Clint replied. "It's the only way to be. It keeps life from being dull."

"Not boring?" Tyna asked, innocently.

"I almost took 'bored to death' too far," Bibi said. "Dull will do nicely."

They joked, had the delicious dinner, then went to bed, after a couple of hours chatting on the porch. In the morning Bibi and Beto left.

Clinton Faraday felt he was luckier than any mere human being had a right to be.

C. D. Moulton's works are available on most major outlets as printed or e-books. CD writes the CD Grimes, PI, mysteries, the Det. Lt. Nick Storie mysteries, the Clint Faraday mysteries, the Flight of the Maita science fiction series, books on orchid culture and many others of many types. Mystery, adventure, intrigue, science fiction, humor, fantasy, paranormal, mild erotica, and factual.

www.ingramcontent.com/pod-product-compliance
Lightning Source LLC
Chambersburg PA
CBHW072205150726
48002CB00014B/1304

*9 7 9 8 2 1 5 5 8 7 6 4 5 *